Who's Afraid of the BIG BAD BOGEY?

To Hayden and Max,
with love
tim

For Max
and Jojo
tom

First published in 2018 by Scholastic Children's Books
Euston House, 24 Eversholt Street, London NW1 1DB
a division of Scholastic Ltd
www.scholastic.co.uk

London ~ New York ~ Toronto ~ Sydney ~ Auckland
Mexico City ~ New Delhi ~ Hong Kong

Text copyright © 2018 Timothy Knapman
Illustrations copyright © 2018 Tom Knight

PB ISBN 978 1407 17976 6

The moral rights of Timothy Knapman
and Tom Knight have been asserted.

Printed in Malaysia

Papers used by Scholastic Children's Books are made from wood grown in sustainable forests.

Who's Afraid of the BIG BAD BOGEY?

Timothy Knapman   Tom Knight

SCHOLASTIC

Once upon a time, in a faraway land… three bogeys lived up the horrid, hairy nose of a massive giant.

Their names were James, Alice and the **Big Bad Bogey**. James and Alice were as sweet as can be.

But the Big Bad Bogey was **very** naughty indeed!
He loved **pulling** on the hairs inside the Giant's
revolting nose and making him sneeze.

One day, the Giant had had enough.

He stuck his finger up his nose
and had a **really good pick.**

"Help!" said James and Alice.
"He's going to pull us out
and eat us!"

But the Big Bad Bogey was bored of living up the Giant's nose. He jumped onto the finger shouting,

YIPPEE!

The Giant was going to eat
the Big Bad Bogey, but he was
SO **big** and SO **bad**

that the Giant flicked him away instead.

As the Big Bad Bogey flew through the air, he sang,

"Who's afraid of the Big Bad Bogey?
The Big Bad Bogey, the Big Bad Bogey?
Who's afraid of the Big Bad Bogey?
Every one of you!"

Then the Big Bad Bogey went **crashing** through the roof of...

GRANDMA'S HOUSE

just as she was about to be eaten by the Wolf...

And he squished the Wolf flat.

Little Red Riding Hood came in and said, "Grandma, what a big **bogey** you've got!"

"All the better to **squish** you with!" said the Big Bad Bogey. "Don't you dare!" said the Woodcutter, waggling his axe.

"Ha ha!" laughed the Big Bad Bogey and he went **bouncing** over to...

just as Goldilocks was about to eat one of the bowls of porridge.

The Big Bad Bogey **bounced** into the first bowl:
"Ouch, too hot!"

Then into the second bowl:
"Ooh, too cold!"

And lastly into the third bowl:
"Mmm, just right."

"I'm not eating that **now!**"
said Goldilocks. "It's got
a **bogey** in it!"

"Ha ha!"

laughed the
Big Bad Bogey and he went
bouncing over to...

CINDERELLA'S HOUSE

just as the Fairy Godmother
was turning a pumpkin
into a carriage.

It was the most **beautiful** carriage there ever was...
until the Big Bad Bogey came **bouncing** in...

and **broke** it to bits.

So Cinderella had to go to the
ball on a **bogey** instead.
"I am **not** happy," she said.

But the Big Bad Bogey didn't care.

"Ha ha!" he laughed as they
went **bouncing** over to...

The Palace

While Cinderella was dancing with the Handsome Prince, the Big Bad Bogey saw a princess about to kiss a frog.

So he went **bouncing** over and squished the frog flat.

"If I'd kissed that frog, he might have turned into a **prince!**" said the Princess. "But you're disgusting and ugly too, so if I kiss **you**, you might turn into my **true love**."

She kissed the Big Bad Bogey, but he just stayed the same.

"I feel **sick** now," said the Princess.

At that very moment, the clock in the palace tower struck midnight, and Cinderella ran away from the ball.

She left her glass slipper behind on the stairs.

The Handsome Prince said, "I will marry the person who fits this slipper."

The Ugly Sisters wanted to try it on, but before they got the chance...

The Big Bad Bogey
bounced into the glass slipper
and it fitted him **perfectly**.

"Will YOU marry me?"
asked the Handsome Prince
with a tender sigh.

"I don't see why not," said the Big Bad Bogey.

"Because you've **spoiled** my story, that's why not!" said Cinderella, storming up to the Big Bad Bogey. She was **very** cross.

"And mine!" said the princess with the frog.

"And mine!" said Goldilocks.

"And mine!" said Little Red Riding Hood.

The Big Bad Bogey looked around at all of their faces.

They were very, VERY upset.

The Big Bad Bogey had been ENORMOUSLY naughty.

He had spoiled EVERYTHING.

And he knew he should feel

VERY ASHAMED INDEED.

But he didn't.

"Ha ha!" laughed the
Big Bad Bogey. And he sang,

"Who's afraid of the Big Bad Bogey?
The Big Bad Bogey, the Big Bad Bogey?
Who's afraid of the Big Bad Bogey?
Every one of you!"

"Yes, I'll marry you," he said to the Handsome Prince.
And they went **bouncing** off into the sunset
to live happily ever after when...

The massive giant picked up the Big Bad Bogey and decided to eat him after all.